D0568812

CUENTO
DE LUZ

With love to my dear friend Don Armenia, a doctor who makes a world of difference.

—Virginia Kroll—

Moon's Messenger

Text © 2015 Virginia Kroll
Illustrations © 2015 Zuzanna Celej
This edition © 2015 Cuento de Luz SL
Calle Claveles, 10 | Urb. Monteclaro | Pozuelo de Alarcón | 28223 | Madrid | Spain
www.cuentodeluz.com

ISBN: 978-84-16147-20-5

Printed by Shanghai Chenxi Printing Co., Ltd. July 2015, print number 1526-8

All rights reserved

FSC
www.fsc.org
MIX
Paper from
responsible sources
FSC® C007923

Moon's Messenger

Virginia Kroll & Zuzanna Celej

Moon sat alone on the beach near her village, watching the sun being gulped whole like a tangerine by a giant's mouth.

Sandpipers scooted along the shore, and a teeny crab dashed by and disappeared into the sand.

Suddenly Moon heard a ripple. She felt a splash. Moon blinked the water away. A great green turtle washed up and braced itself with the back tip of its shell in the wet sand. Moon gasped. She knew how unusual such an encounter was. Of all the sea turtles, greens were the most endangered on earth.

Green Turtle wore a frown and pleaded silently with Moon, who read a sad expression in its golden eyes. "What is it, Turtle? Why are you here?"

The turtle beckoned, *Come*, with its strong front flipper, and, as if it had actually spoken, Moon knew that it wanted to show her something.

She climbed atop its heart-shaped shell. Green Turtle turned and paddled out to sea, rearing up now and then so that Moon could take deep breaths.

First it dove to the depths, and Moon saw the graveyard where dinosaurs and dodos, mammoths and moas, sabre-toothed tigers and passenger pigeons, lay lifeless forever. *These are the extinct ones*, Moon somehow knew.

In the water, the huge reptile was feather light and fast. Moon urged the turtle on and was surprised that she could hold her breath so long.

Underwater, Moon opened her wondering eyes. Black angelfish with silver haloes winged by. Coral polyps pulsated in pink and purple tones. Cowries imitated monsters' toothy mouths, and scallops looked like rows of miniature blue-eyed kittens hiding in dark closets. Skates whizzed by in puffs of sand as squids vanished in inky clouds. Seahorses twined around eel grass and each other, dancing to ocean rhythms. The strands of Moon's light hair flowed long and smooth like seaweed.

Green Turtle began to cruise, and Moon realized that they were coming close to shore. The turtle brought her to a land where branches twisted like intricate mazes and vines crept like serpents over, under, around, and through them. Above the roar of power saws, beautiful beak-heavy birds screeched their protest and monkeys mourned with heart-wrenching howls as trees crashed onto the floor of their rainforest.

Why do they have to take all the trees in one place? Moon wondered. *How will these animals ever live in peace?* A worse thought hit her: *How will they live at all?*

Then Green Turtle traveled to a distant place where once-glistening granite pebbles were blackened with oil. A few lonely gulls with darkened feathers squealed about the otters that used to play with them. Moon didn't know where the oil had come from, but she wondered, *How can people be so careless?*

Next, Green Turtle took Moon to a gulf where motorboats tore up the water hyacinths and scarred manatees' hides as they munched in the shallows of their tropical home. Moon said, "Why can't humans sail their boats in deeper water?"

Green Turtle moved on, and the water grew cold. Moon shivered at the next stop. Even though spring was spreading over the snowy landscape, the north wind kept the air very chilly. Moon hugged her arms around herself and glanced at the shore. A man was setting fur traps for minks and foxes so that he could sell their coats for people to wear.

As Green Turtle turned to continue their journey, Moon noticed a tired polar bear struggling to find an iceberg so it could rest.

Moon felt her own muscles ache, just watching the effort. She had heard that something called *global warming* was ruining polar bears' habitats. "We have to stop all this!" she cried as Green Turtle resumed their journey.

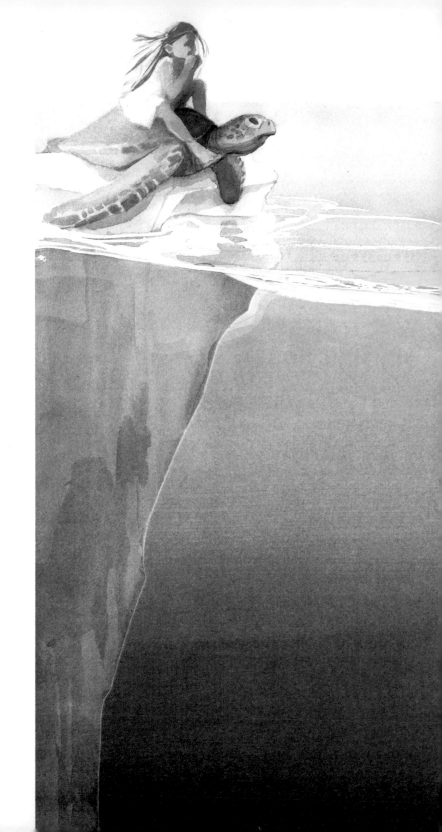

They arrived at a more temperate place. Green Turtle pulled up to a shoreline where a brick building stood. A sign in front announced "Town Meeting Tonight." She could hear angry voices spilling from the windows. People were discussing what to do about the deer that were eating their backyard shrubs and the raccoons that were raiding their trash cans.

"What do they expect?" Moon said. "They steal the creatures' homes and complain when they try to survive!"

Moon patted Green Turtle's shell. She had seen enough.

Green Turtle paddled into the sea, lolling as it munched sea grass while Moon basked atop its back. Green Turtle folded its flippers behind its shell, and Moon used one as a pillow. By now the moon was spilling silver rays onto the gentle waves, and Moon fell asleep to their soothing, rocking rhythm.

She awoke just before dawn in a familiar place and realized, "I'm home." She looked around. The beach was deserted, dark, and peaceful. Moon dismounted, expecting Green Turtle to head back out to sea. Instead, it lumbered further onto land. Heavily it plodded until it seemed that it could move no more. Green Turtle laid its head in the sand and exhaled—hard.

Moon felt her heart sink. "Don't die, don't die, Green Turtle!" she cried.

Suddenly, the turtle raised its head and began pushing sand aside with its back flippers. Furiously it dug to make a hole. Then calmly, it lowered itself, backwards, into the hole. One by one, it laid one hundred round, leathery eggs. Moon could barely catch her breath as she witnessed it. "A miracle," she whispered.

When it had securely covered its treasures, Moon was sure that the corners of Green Turtle's mouth were turned upward at the corners, and its frown was gone. "They will return to sea. I'll protect them," Moon promised. "Every single one of them."

Green Turtle glanced over its shell at Moon. Their eyes exchanged understanding glances before it plodded back to sea, leaving a toboggan-like trail and its message behind it. Just then, Moon saw the horizon brighten, and she felt the mildest of breezes begin to dry her sea-soaked body.

Moon was tired, but she realized there was work to do that could not wait. She wouldn't leave it to others, and it could not wait till she grew up either. She would gather her friends this very morning. For one thing, she would need help fencing in Green Turtle's nest. For another, she had to tell them all about what she had seen and form a plan for stopping it.

As Moon ran home, images of life swam around her mind, while Green Turtle's message swirled within her heart.

Green Sea Turtles

Green sea turtles live in tropical and subtropical oceans around the world. These beautiful creatures are not actually green, but have shells (called carapaces) that come in a range of patterns and colors from olive to brown to black. It is the green fat under their shells that gives them the name "Greens". But the existence of these special turtles is threatened by hunters who kill them for their meat and eggs, propellers that maim them, fishnets that trap them, and development that eliminates their crucial nesting grounds. Despite the fact that these peaceful creatures can live for 80 to 100 years, and swim across oceans to reach the beaches where they lay their eggs, they are now endangered.

It is not too late to save the green sea turtle, along with other animals that call the ocean home. What will you do to help?